3 1994 01107 0510

SANTA ANA PUBLIC LIBRARY
BOOKMOBILE

D0792340

Way Out West

with a Baby!

J ECE EMOTION PICT BK
BROWNLOW, M.
Brownlow, Michael   JUN 2 8 2001
Way out West, with a
    baby! $13.95
BOOKMOBILE 1 31994011070510

Mike Brownlow

Ragged Bears Publishing

Brooklyn, New York • Milborne Wick, Dorset

Way out west and way back then
When skies were fresh and clear,
Cowboys used to take their cows
From there to over here.

They'd drive those cows from sunup
Over desert, over creek,
And the roughest toughest cowboys...

Were Dan and Dom and Deke.

Dan was young and springy
And had long unruly hair,
While skinny Deke talked in a squeak
And Dom looked like a bear.

They'd fight and cuss and scratch and spit;
The worst of them was Dom...
He didn't even send a card
At Christmas to his Mom.

They'd herd those cows for miles all day
Through blizzards, winds and rains,
And rarely see another soul
'Cept passing wagon trains.

But late at night at chow-time
As they ate their meat and bread,
A sound came from the desert
Like a noise to wake the dead!

"Is that a ghost?" asked Dan agog.
The others answered "Nah."
The sound was more familiar.
It grew louder. It went "Waahhh!!"

"It came from over there," said Deke.
Said Dom, "Let's look around."
The cowboys soon stood open-mouthed
Amazed at what they'd found...

For there atop some sage brush
Looking helpless, cold and small,
Was a little crying baby
Swaddled tightly in a shawl.

"A baby! Way out here!" said Dom,
"All tiny, mild and meek,
I guess we'd better pick her up...
Ah shucks... she's sprung a leak!"

"She's wetter than a flood in spring,
And poo!.. will you just smell her?"
And so he took the diaper off...
"Hey guys... this girl's a fella!"

"We gotta clean you up now, son."
The baby gave a shiver.
The cowboys thought and then they dunked
The infant in the river.

They wrapped him in a neckerchief,
And warmed him in his shawl.
But the baby kept on crying
Like a banshee in a squall.

"Ah gee" said Deke, "Ah shucks" said Dom,
"Don't cry now little mite,
'Cause Uncle Dan can do some tricks
To make you feel all right."

"Who, me?" said Dan, "Yeah, you," growled Dom,
But Dan was out of practise.
He tried to stand upon his hands...
And landed in a cactus.

The baby started chuckling
Though only for a while,
So Deke tried pulling faces
But that didn't raise a smile.

"Gee, this baby thing is tough,"
Said Deke amid the din,
"Even though there's three of us
And only one of him."

The cowboys tried to dance and jig
Whilst going "Coochy-coo."
But then the answer came to Dom
...I bet you've guessed it too!

"This little guy is hungry!
That's why he's acting mean."
Said Deke, "D'you think he'd like some steak?
Or maybe he'd like beans?"

"It's milk he wants, you fool!" said Dom,
"We need to git some now.
Dan... pull out all those prickles
And go off and milk a cow."

So soon the night was quiet
As the baby guzzled up,
And drank his fill and finished
What was left inside his cup.

The four sat round the campfire
Underneath the starry skies;
The baby gave a little burp
And rubbed his little eyes.

And then he smiled a gummy smile
And snuggled up to nap,
And soon was dreaming peacefully
On Dom's big manly lap.

Dom scratched his hairy whiskers
And came over kinda calm,
And gazed in wonder at the child
That nestled in his arm.

He rocked the infant quietly
Not knowing what to say,
And something cold in Dom's old heart
Began to melt away.

Then way off in the distance
They heard a rumbling sound.
"Ah shoot!" said Deke, "That's thunder!"
And he spat onto the ground.

The other two, they frowned and snapped,
"Now just hang on a bit.
We gotta raise the baby good,
So Deke... don't cuss or spit!"

Then Dom said "I've been thinking
'Bout this baby and the way
He must have fallen from the wagon train
We saw today."

"We gotta get him to his Mom
And get him to her quick,
'Cause I've a kinda inkling
That she might be worried sick."

Now cowboys know that lightning
Can spook the cattle funny,
And maybe start a stampede
That will cost them lots of money.

"But guys we gotta do the thing
That's right and good," said Dom.
"Let's leave the cows and saddle up...
This baby needs his Mom!"

So off they rode into the night,
The night of inky blue,
And odd to say but half a dozen cattle
Followed too.

Dan was riding on the left
And Deke was on the right,
And in between them there was Dom
Who held the baby tight.

The thunder grew much louder
And it soon came on to rain,
But still they rode determinedly
Toward the wagon train.

Then... CRACKLE! ZAPP! KERBOOM! CRR...ACK!!
The storm was on them now!
The sky lit up as lightning flashed
And barbecued a cow!

Flash floods! Thunder! Rain and hail!
Their horses bucked and reared!
But Dan and Dom and Deke rode on,
Though mightily afeared!

They ducked and dodged the lightning bolts
Yet baby didn't cry,
Until a glob of mud flew up
And hit him in the eye.

"Just hang on little fella,"
Dom's voice was just a croak.
He knew they had to run the storm...
They had to go for broke!

So they galloped fit to bursting
'Til the storm had passed them by,
And as the air began to still
Some smoke rose in the sky.

They rode atop a nearby hill
And peered across the plain,
And as the rays of dawn came up...
They saw the wagon train!

Dom wiped the mud from junior's eyes,
The baby on his knees.
"Look kid... I'll bet your Mom's down there,"
And gave a tender squeeze.

The baby seemed to smile at first
But quickly changed his mood,
And promptly, over Dom's best shirt,
He sicked up all his food.

"No matter son, this thing'll wash.
It really ain't no bother,"
Although he thought, "If not one end,
It comes out of the other!"

They rode towards the wagon train
And who'd you think they saw?
A woman with her arms outstretched...
The little baby's Ma!

She couldn't say a word for tears
As babe returned to Mom.
Said Deke, "He might be hungry, ma'am."
"I <u>know</u> he is!" said Dom.

"Thank God he's safe," the mother sobbed,
No longer in dismay,
And Dom and Dan and Deke discreetly
Wiped a tear away.

"We thought we'd lost him in the storm,"
The baby's father said,
"We searched all over through the night...
We feared he might be dead!"

"Shucks... he was only fooling round,"
Said Dom, "Just having fun.
He thought 'I'm big and tough... let's see
How herding cattle's done!"

The grateful pioneers then fed
The cowhands with some grub,
And after, Dom took off his shirt
And gave the thing a scrub.

But when they came to take their leave
With all their farewells made,
The cowboys went to see the child
Now sleeping in the shade.

"Well, so long kid, we gotta go...
So you take care, y'hear?
'Cause there won't always be three
Guardian cowboys standing near!"

And what became of the baby?

He dreamt of riding on a horse,
And thunder on the plain,
And starry nights and campfires,
And cattle in the rain.

And when he'd done with schooling
And had grown into a man,
He chose to be a cowboy...
Just like Dom and Deke and Dan.

"Now you take good care of your babies, y'hear!"